This book is
the las

Ali Baba

— AND THE —

Forty Thieves

A Parragon Book

Published by
Parragon Books,
Unit 13–17, Avonbridge Trading Estate,
Atlantic Road, Avonmouth, Bristol BS11 9QD

Produced by
The Templar Company plc,
Pippbrook Mill, London Road, Dorking, Surrey RH4 1JE

Designed by Mark Kingsley-Monks

Printed and bound in Italy

ISBN 0-75250-909-8

Ali Baba
— AND THE —
Forty Thieves

Retold by Stephanie Laslett
Illustrated by Helen Cockburn

Far away in the land of Persia there lived a man named Ali Baba. One day he saw a troop of men galloping through the forest. They looked like robbers so he quickly hid in a tree to be safe from harm. The robbers stopped close by and gathered in front of a sheer rock face. Then the Captain called out "Open, Sesame!" and to Ali Baba's great surprise a secret door in the rocks swung open. The Forty Thieves slipped inside and the door closed tight behind them.

Some time later the door swung open once again. The robbers filed out and rode off. Ali Baba was curious. What could be inside that secret cave?

"Open, Sesame!" cried Ali Baba, standing in front of the rock, and soon he found himself behind the door and surrounded by treasure and great riches. He scooped up as much gold as he could carry and headed for home as fast as his feet could carry him.

"What good fortune!" cried his wife. "I must measure this gold at once!"

She borrowed a jar from the wife of Ali Baba's brother, Cassim. "I need to measure something," she explained. But when she returned the jar, Cassim's wife discovered a piece of gold lying in the bottom.

"Ali Baba must be very rich," she told her husband. "He does not count his money — he *measures* it!"

Then Cassim was very jealous and he went to Ali Baba and asked where he had found so much gold. Now Ali Baba was a good man and he decided to share his secret with his brother.

But Cassim was a greedy man and he was determined to take all the treasure for himself. So the next morning he went to the forest alone.

"Open, Sesame!" he cried. Soon he had gathered as much treasure as he could carry. But when he came to leave, he had forgotten the secret password and could not get out! He was trapped!

Soon he heard a trampling of hooves outside the cave. The robbers had arrived! As they marched into the cave, Cassim tried to hide but with cries of rage they saw him and fell upon him with their sabres.

And so greedy Cassim died and his body was left amidst the treasure as a lesson to anyone else who might be so foolish as to enter the robber's den.

Later that night Ali Baba went to the cave to collect more gold, but the first thing he saw was the body of his dead brother. He realised at once what must have happened and, loading the body on to his donkey, he set off for his home as quickly as possible.

Ali Baba returned through the forest, much saddened by this new turn of events. He explained all that had happened to Morgiana, his maidservant, and asked for her help.

"You must find someone who can sew the four quarters of Cassim's body together again," he ordered. "Then we can bury him properly."

Early the next day Morgiana went to an old cobbler near the town gate.

"Come with me, old man," she said. "I have some work for you to do." She blindfolded him and led him to Ali Baba's house and there he stitched together the parts of Cassim's body.

When the job was done, Morgiana once again blindfolded the cobbler and led him back to his stall. She was sure he would never be able to find the house again and so their secret would be safe. But the old man was cunning. He knew the city so well that he could tell by the feel of the cobbles just where he had gone.

The next day the Forty Thieves returned to their cave and saw at once that the body had gone.

"Somebody else must know our secret!" cried the Captain. "He must be found and killed!"

So he ordered one of the robbers to visit the town and try to discover who this intruder might be.

The first person that the robber saw as he entered the town gate was the old cobbler stitching at his stall.

"Old man," whispered the robber. "Have you noticed any strange happenings in this town recently?"

The old man nodded slowly as the robber passed him a piece of gold.

"Why, last night I was blindfolded and taken to stitch together a dead body," he hissed, "and if you were to give me another piece of gold I might just remember how to find the house where it happened, as long as I am blindfolded again." Soon they were standing outside Ali Baba's home.

The robber marked a cross on the door with a piece of chalk so that they would be able to find it easily the next day and he returned to the cave, well pleased with his work.

The Captain now worked out a clever plan to trick Ali Baba. He bought forty leather oil jars and hid each of his men inside each one. The jars were loaded onto donkeys and, disguising himself as an oil merchant, the Captain set off for the town.

When he arrived outside the door with the cross there was Ali Baba himself sitting in the sunshine.

"I have brought this oil to sell in the market tomorrow," explained the Robber Captain. "But I need somewhere to stay for the night. Can you help me?"

Ali Baba was a kind man and he invited the Captain inside.

The oil jars were offloaded into Ali Baba's yard and the Captain quickly whispered to each of his men.

"I will call for you later so be ready for my command." Then he went inside to eat with Ali Baba.

Later that evening Morgiana was passing through the yard when she heard a voice from inside one of the jars. "Is is time now?" it said.

Morgiana was astonished but knew at once that there must be a plot afoot to murder Ali Baba.

"That oil merchant must be the Robber Captain," she decided.

She returned to the jars with a large pot of boiling oil which she poured it into each one until every robber was dead.

In the dead of night, when he thought everyone else in the house must be asleep, the Captain stole quietly into the yard and tried to rouse his men. But when he found that each one was dead he realised that his plan had been discovered.

In great fear, he ran from the yard. Back in his cave the Captain wept aloud at the loss of his Forty Thieves, but soon he had hatched a new plan to repay Ali Baba once and for all.

The Captain disguised himself as a cloth merchant and he set up a stall right opposite Ali Baba's house.

He sold fine linen and beautiful silks and soon Ali Baba came across the street to look at the magnificent display of goods.

He did not recognise the Captain and soon they had become quite friendly. The Robber's plan was working well!

"You must come and eat with me this evening," insisted Ali Baba. "I would like you to meet my son."

"We have a guest for dinner," Ali Baba told Morgiana. "Prepare the best food in the house."

But when Morgiana saw the visitor arrive at the door she recognised him at once as the Robber Captain, and feared again for Ali Baba's life.

"He is in great danger," she told the cook, "so you must help me in my plan. I am going to dance before they eat and I will carry a dagger in my belt. You play a beat on the tabor and together we will save our master."

So they prepared themselves and went upstairs to dance before Ali Baba, his son and their guest.

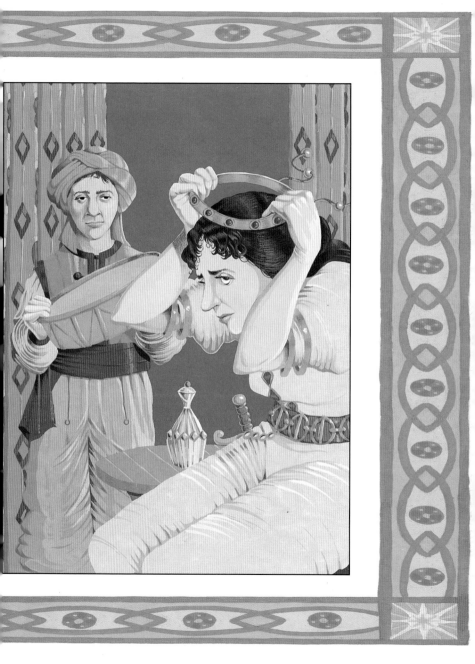

"Enter, Morgiana," said Ali Baba. "Come and dance before our honoured visitor. We would welcome some entertainment before our meal."

So the cook beat upon the tabor and Morgiana began to dance to the rhythm of the drum. She whirled around the room and as she drew near the Robber Captain she caught a glimpse of a knife hidden inside his coat. She had been right to suspect him. He was going to murder Ali Baba!

The beat of the tabor grew louder and Morgiana danced ever closer to the Captain. Suddenly she grasped her dagger and, before anyone had time to realise what she meant to do, she had plunged it deep into the Robber's black heart.

"He is no cloth merchant, master," cried Morgiana as Ali Baba sat rooted with shock. "He is the Robber Captain and he planned to kill you." Quickly she showed Ali Baba the knife hidden inside the Robber's coat.

Ali Baba was so grateful to the brave and clever maidservant for saving his life that he agreed to let her marry his son, for they had fallen in love some weeks before. Morgiana was overjoyed and so the wedding was celebrated in much splendour.

In time Ali Baba shared the secret of the Robber's cave with his son and Morgiana and as the years passed, Ali Baba's son passed on the secret password to his own children. They in turn passed it to their own and so the family of Ali Baba lived in great wealth and happiness for the rest of their days.

Ali Baba and the Forty Thieves belongs to
one of the greatest story collections of all time:
The Tales of the Arabian Nights, also known as
The Book of One Thousand and One Nights.
These stories were first written many hundreds
of years ago and include *Aladdin and the
Wonderful Lamp*,
The Voyages of Sinbad the Sailor
and *The Magic Carpet*.
They were originally told by the beautiful
Princess Scheherezade to the suspicious Prince
of Tartary, who had threatened to behead her at
daybreak. But her tales were so exciting that,
as the sun rose, he longed to hear how they
ended and so pardoned her life for one more
day, until after one thousand and
one nights Scheherezade had won
his trust and his heart.